The Secret Weapon

Text © Nicci Crowther 1998

Illustrations © Tony Blundell 1998

First published in Great Britain in 1998 by

Macdonald Young Books

足球隊的祕密武器

Nicci Crowther 著

Tony Blundell 繪

刊欣媒體營造工作室 譯

Chapter One

Every Sunday morning Leo went to the park to play **football**. Lots of his friends came too.

Billy liked to play in **goal**. He was great at leaping **sideways** into the air, although he didn't always **manage to** stop the ball.

Zoë was great at **tackling**. Sometimes she kicked the other players' legs, but she always said sorry.

第一章

　　每個星期天早上，李奧都會到公園踢足球，他的許多朋友也會來一起玩。

　　比利喜歡守球門，他擅長騰空側躍，雖然他並不是每次都能擋得住球。

　　若伊擅於攔截，有時她會踢到其他球員的腳，但她都會道歉。

football [`fut,bɔl] 图 足球
goal [gol] 图 球門
sideways [`saɪd,wez] 副 側面地
manage to （排除困難）成功地做…
tackle [`tækl] 動 攔截，搶球

JASON

3

Tony was very good at **passing** — but not always to the right team.

Rani was very fast but she had a habit of **tripping** up over her shoelaces.

Leo liked to play **up front**, and sometimes he even managed to **score** a goal. He was very good at **celebrating**.

While the kids were playing football, their mums and dads would read the papers or take the dog for a walk. They took turns each week to be the **referee**. Zoë's mum, Sandra, was the best ref because she knew all the **rules** and never let anyone **argue**.

東尼精於傳球──不過，不一定會傳到該傳的那隊。

蘭妮跑得很快，可是常常被自己的鞋帶絆倒。

李奧喜歡打前鋒的位置，有時還能射門得分，而他也很會鼓舞士氣。

pass [pæs] 勔 傳球

trip [trɪp] 勔 絆倒《up》

up front （球場的）前面[中央]的位置

score [skor] 勔 得分

celebrate [ˋsɛləˌbret] 勔 歡鬧

當孩子們踢足球時，他們的父母就在一旁看報紙或遛狗。家長們每週輪流當裁判，而若伊的媽媽——珊卓拉——是最好的裁判，因為她懂所有的規則，而且從未讓比賽過程發生爭議。

referee [ˌrɛfəˋri] 名 裁判
rule [rul] 名 規則
argue [ˋɑrgju] 動 爭議

One Sunday, after the final whistle, a man **strolled** over to the crowd of muddy children, dogs and parents.

"My name's Harry Jones," he said. "I **manage** a football team called the Park Rangers. We'd like to **challenge** you to a **match**. Five-a-side."

"Done!" said Sandra. "**Turn up** here in three weeks' time — and may the best team win!"

有一個星期天，就在球賽結束的哨音響起後，一位先生朝這群滿身泥巴的小孩、狗兒和家長晃了過來。

　　「我的名字叫做哈里‧瓊斯。」他說。「我帶領一支足球隊，叫公園騎警隊，我們想和你們進行一場比賽，每隊五人。」

　　「沒問題！」珊卓拉說。「三個禮拜之後在這兒進行比賽，最好的一隊將會獲勝！」

stroll [strol] 勔 閒逛
manage [`mænɪdʒ] 勔 管理
challenge [`tʃælɪndʒ] 勔 挑戰
match [mætʃ] 图 比賽
turn up　發生；出現

When Harry Jones had gone, everyone sat outside the café and **worked out** the **squad**. They would call themselves the Reds, because everyone had a red T shirt. Billy would go in goal. Zoë and Tony would **defend**. Leo and Rani would be **strikers**.

哈里・瓊斯離開後，大家坐在咖啡館外推演隊形。他們自稱為紅人隊，因為每個人都有一件紅色 T 恤。比利守球門、若伊和東尼防守、李奧及蘭妮當前鋒負責進攻。

work out　推算
squad [skwɑd] 名 隊
defend [dɪ`fɛnd] 動 防守
striker [`straɪkɚ] 名 前鋒

"**D**o you think we can **beat** the Park Rangers?" asked Billy, as he **munched** on a second slice of cake. "They might be really good."

"**Nonsense**!" said Sandra. "With a bit of practice, you lot will be a **match** for anyone."

So all next week they practiced.

「你們認為我們能夠擊敗公園騎警隊嗎？」比利一邊大聲地嚼著第二塊蛋糕一邊問。「他們可能很厲害。」

　　「胡說！」珊卓拉說。「只要練習一下，你們的實力足夠和任何隊伍競爭。」

　　於是接下來的一整個禮拜，他們都在練習。

beat [bit] 動 擊敗
munch [mʌntʃ] 動 大聲地咀嚼
nonsense [ˋnɑnsɛns] 感 胡說
match [mætʃ] 名 旗鼓相當的對手《for》

Leo and Rani met up in the park after school to practice **penalties**, although Rani's dog kept running off with the ball.

Zoë practiced tackles on her baby sister, until the baby fell over and cried once too often.

李奧和蘭妮放學後在公園見面，練習罰球，可是蘭妮的狗一直把球叼走。

　　若伊要他的小妹和他練習攔截，直到小妹跌倒，放聲大哭了起來。

penalty [`pɛnḷtɪ] 名 罰球

Tony practiced **headers** against his bedroom wall, until the neighbors **came round** to **complain**.

Billy thought the best thing he could do was **build up** his strength, so he practiced making chocolate cakes.

東尼對著臥室的牆壁練習頂球，直到鄰居過來抱怨。

比利認為最好的方法是增強自己的體力，所以他練習的是做巧克力蛋糕。

header [ˋhɛdɚ] 名 頂球
come round 來訪 (= come around)
complain [kəmˋplen] 動 抱怨
build up 增強

Chapter Two

Leo hoped all the practice was doing them good. But when they started playing next Sunday, he wasn't so sure. For the first time, everyone **noticed** how many goals Billy let in, and how many times Zoë miskicked the ball. Tony kept giving the ball to the other team, and Leo **missed** three times in front of an open goal.

第二章

　　李奧希望這一切的練習都能對他們有所幫助。但是，當他們第二個星期天開始踢球時，他可就沒那麼有把握了。這是第一次大家注意到比利讓對手進了多少球，若伊沒踢中幾球，而東尼一直把球傳給對方球隊，李奧則是三次在無人防備的球門前錯失了射門的機會。

notice [`notɪs] 勔 注意到
miss [mɪs] 勔 錯失

"**W**e'll get **hammered at this rate**," said Rani.

After the game, they sat outside the café as usual, but everyone was very quiet. Even Billy had lost his **appetite**.

"**W**inning isn't everything," said Rani, but she didn't sound like she really meant it.

"**Cheer up**," said Sandra. "You can't **give up** already."

"What we need is a secret **weapon**," said Leo. "Something that will make all the difference."

「照這種程度看來，我們一定會被打得落花流水。」蘭妮說。

　　打完球之後，他們像往常一樣坐在咖啡館外，只是大夥兒都很安靜，連比利也沒了胃口。

hammer [ˋhæmɚ] 勔 把…打得落花流水
at this rate　以這種情形看來
appetite [ˋæpəˌtaɪt] 名 胃口

「贏球不是一切。」蘭妮說，不過聽起來並不像真心話。

「振作一點啦！」珊卓拉說。「你們已經不能棄權了。」

「我們需要的是祕密武器。」李奧說。「某種能讓我們截然不同的東西。」

cheer up　振作
give up　放棄
weapon [`wɛpən] 名 武器

"**S**omething — or someone."

There was a long **silence**, while everyone had a think.

Then Billy said, "I could ask my **cousin** Jason to play for us, only..."

「某種東西——或者某個人。」

有一段很長的沉默，大夥兒都在想著這個問題。

然後比利說：「我可以請我表哥傑森來替我們打球，只是……」

silence [ˋsaɪləns] 图 沉默
cousin [ˋkʌzn̩] 图 堂（表）兄弟姊妹

"Is he any good?" the others **chorused**.

"Well yes," said Billy, "he's a footballing **genius**. The only trouble is..."

「他很厲害嗎？」其他人異口同聲地問。

「對啊！」比利說。「他是個足球天才，唯一的麻煩是……」

chorus [ˋkorəs] 動 齊聲說

genius [ˋdʒinjəs] 名 天才

"**A** footballing genius? What do you mean?"

"He can find the **back** of the **net** with his eyes closed," **explained** Billy. "He could **take on** the whole of Liverpool and Manchester United put together, but the thing is..."

"Go for it!" said Sandra. "If he's half as good as you say, we can't do without him."

「足球天才？什麼意思啊？」

「他閉著眼睛也能射球入門。」比利解釋著，「利物浦與曼徹斯特兩隊加起來也打不過他呢！不過問題在於⋯⋯」

「去找他吧！」珊卓拉說。「如果他有你說的一半好，我們就不能沒有他。」

back [bæk] 图 背部，深處
net [nɛt] 图 網（此處指球門）
explain [ɪk`splen] 勔 解釋
take on 向⋯挑戰

Chapter Three

Everyone **looked forward to** meeting Jason next Sunday. When he arrived, he was wearing a **brand-new strip** with his name on the back and the most expensive boots you could buy.

"I'll play up front," said Jason, running on the **spot**. "Just make sure I get the ball and the goals will follow."

第三章

　　接下來的這個星期天，大家都期待著要見見傑森。他抵達時，身上穿著嶄新的足球服，背上绣了名字，腳上穿著最昂貴的球鞋。

　　「我來踢前鋒。」傑森邊說邊跑到定位。「只要我拿到球，保證能射門得分。」

look forward to　期盼
brand-new [`bræn`nju] 形 嶄新的
strip [strɪp] 名 （足球選手穿的）制服
spot [spɑt] 名 （某特定的）地點

From the **kick-off**, Jason **dribbled** round three players and **lobbed** the **keeper**. Two minutes later he struck a **curler** into the top corner. His third goal was a bicycle kick from the half-way line. Billy had been right. Jason was a footballing genius.

There was only one problem. A big problem. Jason got very **cross** when anyone else tried to join in.

開球後，傑森運球繞過三名球員，吊球越過守門員得分。兩分鐘後，他踢了一個曲球，射進球門頂端的角落。第三球，他倒掛金鈎，從中線射門得分。比利說得沒錯，傑森是個足球天才。

　　只有一個問題——一個大問題。只要其他人想要參與，傑森就會很不高興。

kick-off [`kɪk͵ɔf] 图 開球
dribble [`drɪbḷ] 動 運球，盤球
lob [lɑb] 動 吊球
keeper [`kipɚ] 图 守門員
curler [`kɝlɚ] 图 曲球
cross [krɔs] 形 不高興的

When Rani picked up a **loose** ball on the **wing**, Jason screamed, "To me! Over to me!" When she tripped up over her shoelace, Jason called her an idiot.

When the other team scored a goal, Jason **swore** at Billy and said he was a useless **goalie**.

蘭妮在側翼接到一個誤傳的球，傑森大叫著：「給我！傳過來給我！」當蘭妮被自己的鞋帶絆倒時，傑森罵她是個笨蛋。

　　而對手得分時，傑森對著比利破口大罵，說他是個沒用的守門員。

loose [lus] 形 未被束縛的，自由的
wing [wɪŋ] 名 邊鋒
swear [swɛr] 動 咒罵《at》
　（過去式 swore [swor]）
goalie [`golɪ] 名 守門員
　(= goalkeeper [`gol͵kipɚ])

He even tackled Leo for the ball when they were on the same team.

And the more Jason shouted at them, the more they struggled for breath and their feet got **muddled** up.

After the game, nobody went to the café. They didn't want to listen to Jason going on about what a **crummy** team they were.

而當李奧和他同隊時，他甚至為了搶球把李奧絆倒。

　　傑森越對他們吼叫，他們越緊張，腳上的球就踢得越糟。

　　比賽結束後，沒有人到咖啡館去。他們不想聽傑森繼續批評他們是個多麼差勁的球隊。

muddle [`mʌdl̩] 動 弄糟《up》
crummy [`krʌmɪ] 形 不好的

As they were walking home, Tony said to Leo, "I wish Jason didn't have to play with us."

"Me too," said Leo. "If only we didn't need a secret weapon."

"But we're useless without him."

They stared **glumly** down at the mud caking on their boots. Their whole bodies felt **heavy**.

走在回家的路上，東尼對李奧說：「我真希望傑森不要和我們一起踢球。」

「我也是，」李奧說著，「如果我們不需要祕密武器就好了。」

「可是我們沒有他又不行。」

他們悶悶不樂地看著靴子上厚厚的一層泥巴，整個人感到沉重無比。

glumly [ˋglʌmlɪ] 副 悶悶不樂地
heavy [ˋhɛvɪ] 形 沉重的

Later that week, everyone in the football team met round at Zoë and Sandra's house. Billy brought a cake he'd made, so they could all build up their strength.

"Do you want to go to the park for some more practice?" asked Sandra.

But nobody had the heart for football.

"What's the point?" **muttered** Zoë. "It's no fun any more."

過了幾天，球隊的成員到若伊及珊卓拉家聚會。比利帶來他自己做的蛋糕，好讓大家增強體力。

　　「你們要到公園再練習一會兒嗎？」珊卓拉問。

　　可是沒有人有心情談足球。

　　「有什麼意思呢？」若伊抱怨著，「再也不好玩了。」

mutter [`mʌtɚ] 勔 抱怨

"I tried to warn you about Jason," said Billy.

"It's not your **fault**," said Leo. "At least you're good at making cake."

They all took another slice and watched a **cartoon** on TV.

「我有試過要警告你們傑森的問題。」比利說。

「那不是你的錯。」李奧說。「至少你很會做蛋糕。」

他們一片一片吃著蛋糕，邊看電視卡通。

fault [fɔlt] 名 過錯；責任
cartoon [kɑr`tun] 名 卡通

Chapter Four

On Sunday morning, Leo woke up early
with an **empty** feeling in his stomach. He
should have been looking forward to the match,
but he knew they were all going to play badly,
and Jason would shout at them.

第四章

　　星期天早上，李奧很早就醒來了，覺得肚子空空的。他原本應該期待著今天的球賽，不過他知道他們會表現得很差，然後傑森就會對他們大吼大叫。

empty [`ɛmptɪ] 形 空的

When Leo and the others got to the park, the Rangers were already waiting. They looked huge, and their legs were as thick as tree trunks. Jason had a new pair of **shin-pads** and a **plaster** across his nose like **athletes** on TV.

當李奧和其他的人到達公園時，騎警隊已經在那兒等著了。他們看起來是那麼高大，每個人的腿都有樹幹的三倍那麼粗。傑森戴著新的小腿護墊、鼻子上貼了一塊繃帶，就像電視上的運動員一樣。

shin [ʃɪn] 图 脛骨
pad [pæd] 图 護墊
plaster [`plæstɚ] 图 絆創膏
athlete [`æθlit] 图 運動員

With Jason playing up front, Leo had to be a **substitute**. He **huddled** in his coat on the **touchline**, trying to keep warm.

The whistle blew and the Reds kicked off.

Straight away Jason got the ball. He **swerved** round the first **defender**, **chipped** the ball past the second and then ran on to **belt** it into the back of the net. ONE-NIL. Jason **punched** the air and **flashed** a smile at the little crowd of mums and dads.

由於傑森要打前鋒的位置，李奧只好在旁邊當候補。他站在邊線上，緊緊裹著外套保暖。

　　哨音響起了，由紅人隊開球。

　　傑森立刻拿到球，他閃過第一位防守者，切球穿過第二位防守者，然後繼續跑著，將球猛地一踢進網。一比零。傑森在空中舞動著拳頭，並向群集的家長展露出笑容。

substitute [`sʌbstəˌtjut] 名 候補

huddle [`hʌdl̩] 動 蜷縮身體

touchline [`tʌtʃˌlaɪn] 名 邊線

swerve [swɝv] 動 偏離

defender [dɪ`fɛndɚ] 名 防守者

chip [tʃɪp] 動 削球，切球

belt [bɛlt] 動 猛打

punch [pʌntʃ] 動 用拳猛擊

flash [flæʃ] 動 閃現

Leo sank deeper into his coat. He noticed the Park Rangers **whispering** to each other and looking at Jason.

As soon as the game restarted, the biggest two Rangers ran over to Jason and stood right beside him. Whenever he tried to **dart** away, they followed closely. They were going to **mark** Jason out of the game.

李奧整個人窩在外套裡。他注意到公園騎警隊的隊員看著傑森，彼此竊竊私語。

　　比賽再度展開時，最高大的兩名騎警隊球員跑向傑森，守在他的旁邊。每當傑森想要猛衝，他們就緊跟不放。他們打算盯住傑森，不讓他踢球。

whisper [`hwɪspɚ] 勔 竊竊私語
dart [dɑrt] 勔 猛衝
mark [mɑrk] 勔 盯住

Before long one of the Rangers had the ball near the Reds' goal.

"Tackle!" screamed Jason. Zoë **lunged** in, but the Rangers player **skipped** over her **outstretched** leg and took **aim**.

"Save it!" screamed Jason. Billy leapt into the air and missed. ONE-ALL. "Call yourself a goalie?" Jason **sneered** as Billy picked himself up out of the mud.

不久後，騎警隊的一名球員運球接近紅人隊的球門。

「抄球！」傑森叫著。若伊衝了過去，但是騎警隊的球員越過她伸出的腳，射門。

「擋住球！」傑森大叫。比利跳到半空中，不過撲了個空。一比一。「你這也叫守門員嗎？」比利從泥堆中爬了起來，傑森嘲笑他。

lunge [lʌndʒ] 動 衝入
skip [skɪp] 動 跳過
outstretched [aut`strɛtʃt] 形 伸展開的
aim [em] 名 目標
sneer [snɪr] 動 嘲笑

53

On the touchline, Leo turned away so he didn't have to watch any more.

Before Rani kicked off again, Jason **hissed**, "Play it straight to me." But she got nervous and kicked it to one of the Park Rangers. Then she fell over her shoelace.

"Fool!" **yelled** Jason. "Look what you've gone and done!"

邊線這端，李奧轉身離開，不想再看下去了。

蘭妮再次開球之前，傑森口氣不好地對她說：「把球直接傳給我。」但是她太緊張了，反而把球踢給騎警隊的球員，然後被自己的鞋帶絆倒。

「笨蛋！」傑森大聲叫喊，「看妳做的好事！」

hiss [hɪs] 動 發出噓聲
yell [jɛl] 動 喊叫

The Park Rangers passed the ball between them up the **field** and **slotted** it neatly under Billy's **diving** body. TWO-ONE.

"You're the worst goalie in the history of the world ever!" Jason screamed at Billy.

公園騎警隊在場上把球傳來傳去，俐落地從比利俯衝的身體下方射球進門。二比一。

「你真是世界上有史以來最差勁的守門員哪！」傑森對著比利大吼大叫。

field [fild] 名 球場

slot [slɑt] 動 嵌入

dive [daɪv] 動 俯衝

The more Jason screamed at the other Reds, the worse they got. Rani actually ran away from the ball so she couldn't be **blamed** for anything. Tony **mistimed** a tackle and gave away a penalty. THREE-ONE.

At **half-time** they **trudged** off the field wishing they'd stayed at home in their nice warm beds.

傑森越是向紅人隊的其他隊員叫囂，他們就打得越差。蘭妮乾脆丟下球不管，那她就不必再挨罵了。東尼在不當的時機抄球，讓對方獲得罰球的機會。三比一。

中場休息時間，他們拖著沉重的腳步走下球場，多麼希望自己是待在家中溫暖的被窩裡啊！

blame [blem] 動 責罵《for》
mistime [mɪsˋtaɪm] 動 弄錯…時機
half-time [ˋhæf͵taɪm] 名 中場休息時間
trudge [trʌdʒ] 動 步履沉重地行走

"**Y**ou're all completely useless!" shouted Jason at the rest of the team. "I've never played with such a **bunch** of **wimps**."

"So much for our secret weapon," muttered Billy as Leo **handed** him a drink.

「你們根本一點兒用處也沒有！」傑森對著他的隊友咆哮起來，「我從沒和這樣一群沒用的人打過球。」

　　「這就是我們的祕密武器！」李奧遞給比利一杯飲料，比利向他抱怨著。

bunch [bʌntʃ] 名 群，夥(= group)
wimp [wɪmp] 名 懦弱的人
hand [hænd] 動 將⋯交給⋯

Chapter Five

The second half started the way the first half left off. Zoë, Rani and Tony hardly got a touch of the ball. Only once did Jason manage to break free from his **markers**. He did a quick side-step, **swivelled** on the ball and **cracked** it into the back of the net. THREE-TWO.

第五章

　　下半場球賽開始，情況和上半場一樣。若伊、蘭妮和東尼幾乎無法碰到球。傑森只有一次成功地擺脫盯著他的對手。他迅速橫跨一步，把球一鈎，啪地一聲踢進網中。三比二。

marker [ˈmɑrkɚ] 名 盯哨者
swivel [ˈswɪvl̩] 動 鈎轉
crack [kræk] 動 使發出啪嗒聲

"You see!" Jason shouted. "I have to do all the work around here." The Rangers' players gave Jason an evil look. One of them **nodded** to the other.

As soon as the Rangers kicked off again, Jason was given some space. He **collected** the ball and set off toward goal. **In a flash** the Rangers crowded round him. One of them gave a **hefty** kick, and it wasn't **aimed** at the ball.

"Ow! My leg!" Jason was **writhing** around on the ground **clutching** his ankle.

The referee's whistle blew. "Penalty to the Reds."

Only Jason wasn't in any fit state to take it. "My leg!" he **sobbed**, rocking back and forth. "It hurts!" Some of the parents hurried on to the **pitch** and helped him **limp** away.

"Get your coat off, Leo," said Sandra. "You're on!"

「你們看看！」傑森叫著，「我一個人要做所有的事。」騎警隊的球員不懷好意地看了傑森一眼，其中一人還對另一個人點點頭。

騎警隊再次開球了，傑森有機可乘。他拿到球並向球門挺進。一瞬間，騎警隊的球員紛紛湧向他，其中一人用力一踢，但他瞄準的目標不是球。

nod [nɑd] 動 點頭
collect [kə`lɛkt] 動 拿來
in a flash 轉瞬間
hefty [`hɛftɪ] 形 大而重的
aim [em] 動 瞄準《at》

「喔！我的腳。」傑森抱著腳踝在地上翻滾。

裁判的哨音響起。「由紅人隊罰球。」

只是傑森的情況根本無法踢罰球。「我的腳！」他一邊哭，一邊來回擺動著受傷的腳。「好痛喲！」有些家長趕忙衝到球場上來，扶著傑森一拐一拐地離開。

「脫掉外套，李奧。」珊卓拉說，「你上場！」

writhe [raɪð] 動 翻滾
clutch [klʌtʃ] 動 緊握
sob [sɑb] 動 啜泣
pitch [pɪtʃ] 名 位置
limp [lɪmp] 動 一拐一拐地走

Leo ran to the others. "Who's taking the penalty?" he asked.

"You are."

Leo stretched his arms and legs and walked up to the penalty spot. The Rangers' goalkeeper looked very big. The goal looked very small. Leo took a short run up and hammered the ball as hard as he could.

李奧跑向其他隊友，「誰來踢罰球？」他問。

「你啊！」

李奧舒展手腳，走向罰球位置。騎警隊的守門員看起來非常高大，球門卻看起來很小。李奧助跑一小段距離，然後使勁一踢。

"GOAL!" THREE-THREE. The rest of the team raced toward Leo, and **thumped** him on the back.

He could hear Sandra's voice from the touchline, "Come on now! Ten minutes left. Only one more goal. You can do it!"

「射門得分！」三比三。隊友們奔向李奧，重重地搥著他的背。

他聽見珊卓拉的聲音從邊線處傳來，「加油！剩十分鐘，只要再進一球你們就贏了。你們做得到的！」

thump [θʌmp] 動 重擊

Chapter Six

The Park Rangers kicked off again. Leo tried to keep up with the ball, but the Rangers were very fast and strong.

Tony dived in for a tackle and missed.

"Unlucky!" shouted Leo.

Zoë closed in on the Rangers' striker but he passed the ball before she reached her.

第六章

　　公園騎警隊再度開球。李奧努力追著球，可是騎警隊跑得又快又激烈。

　　東尼衝入對方陣線想抄球，不過失敗了。

　　「運氣不好！」李奧大叫。

　　若伊逼近騎警隊的前鋒，但是他在若伊靠近前就把球傳走了。

"Good try!" shouted Leo.

A Rangers player fired the ball toward goal. Billy took a flying leap — and he caught it!

"Well played!" came Sandra's shout from the touchline.

「試得好！」李奧又叫著。

一名騎警隊的球員將球往球門一射，比利縱身一躍——他截住那個球了！

「漂亮！」珊卓拉在邊線處大聲叫著。

Quickly Billy threw the ball out to Rani who danced up the wing and **slid** the ball inside to Tony. Tony turned and passed, and **for once** Leo was right there in front of the goal. The Rangers goalie rushed out.

比利很快地把球丟給在邊鋒手舞足蹈的蘭妮，蘭妮再將球向內傳給東尼。東尼轉身傳球，剛巧李奧就站在球門前。騎警隊的守門員衝了出來。

slide [slaɪd] 勔 滑
for once　僅此一次

"I can't miss," thought Leo. But he did. In his hurry, Leo hit the ball with the side of his boot. Instead of **rocketing** forward, it swerved sideways into the path of a defender who stuck out a foot. The goalie tried to change direction and fell **sprawling** in the mud, and the ball **spun** off the defender's boot and into the goal. FOUR-THREE!

「我不能失誤，」李奧心想，但是他還是失誤了。匆忙之中，李奧用鞋子的側邊將球踢了出去。這一球不是直線前衝，而是轉了個彎，繞過一位伸出一腳來防守的對方球員。騎警隊的守門員想要轉向攔截這個球，卻四腳朝天跌在泥堆中，球便從防守者的鞋邊滾進了球門。四比三！

rocket [ˋrɑkɪt] 動 （像火箭般）直衝
sprawl [sprɔl] 動 四肢伸開平躺
spin [spɪn] 動 旋轉
　　（過去式 spun [spʌn]）

After that, all the Reds had to do was to **hang on** till the end of the game. As the minutes **ticked** by, they played better and better. And the Rangers played worse and worse.

Finally the ref blew his whistle.

The Reds had won.

Harry Jones was the first to **congratulate** the team.

"I thought we had you beaten," he said. "But we didn't **reckon with** your secret weapon." He **patted** Leo's shoulder. "What an **inspiration**!"

接下來，紅人隊所要做的便是堅守到球賽結束。時間一分一秒地過去，他們表現得越來越好，而騎警隊卻表現得越來越差。

　　終於，裁判的哨音響起。

　　紅人隊贏了。

hang on　堅持

tick [tɪk] 動 滴答地響

哈里・瓊斯第一個來向他們道賀。

「我原本以為我們贏定你們了，」他說，「沒想到你們有個祕密武器。」他拍拍李奧的肩膀，「多虧有你鼓舞大家的士氣！」

congratulate [kən`grætʃə,let] 動 向…道賀
reckon [`rɛkən] 動 計算；考慮
　　reckon with... 把…列入考慮
pat [pæt] 動 輕拍
inspiration [,ɪnspə`reʃən] 名 鼓舞他人的人

"**S**ecret weapons indeed!" **chuckled** Sandra, handing round some of Billy's home-made chocolate cake.

"Yeah," said Leo. "Who needs them?"

「的確是祕密武器呢！」珊卓拉一邊開心地笑著，一邊遞給他們比利自己做的巧克力蛋糕。

「是啊！」李奧說。「誰需要什麼祕密武器啊？」

chuckle [`tʃʌkl] 勔 咯咯笑

英語發音

黃正興編著

想要說一口又溜又標準的
英語嗎？
想要知道怎麼樣把英文歌
唱得更正確好聽嗎？

畫藝百科系列（入門篇）

一共26冊，每冊定價250元

全球公認最好的一套藝術叢書
讓你在實際觀摩、操作中
學會每一種作畫技巧
享受揮灑彩筆的樂趣與成就感

§ 油畫 § 人體畫 § 靜物畫 § 色鉛筆

§ 畫花世界 § 光與影的秘密

§ 選擇主題 § 風景油畫 § 噴畫

§ 動物畫 § 繪畫色彩學 § 建築之美

§ 繪畫入門 § 水彩畫 § 肖像畫

§ 風景畫 § 粉彩畫 § 海景畫

§ 人體解剖 § 創意水彩 § 如何畫素描

§ 名畫臨摹 § 透視 § 混色

§ 素描的基礎與技法 § 壓克力畫

國家圖書館出版品預行編目資料

足球隊的祕密武器 = The secret weapon / Nicci
　Crowther 著；Tony Blundell 繪；刊欣媒體營造
　工作室譯 ．—初版．——臺北市：三民，民88
　　面；　公分
　ISBN 957–14–3013–7 (平裝)

1.英國語言—讀本

805.18　　　　　　　　　　　　88004024

網際網路位址　http://www.sanmin.com.tw

ⓒ 足 球 隊 的 祕 密 武 器

著作人	Nicci Crowther
繪圖者	Tony Blundell
譯　者	刊欣媒體營造工作室
發行人	劉振強
著作財產權人	三民書局股份有限公司 臺北市復興北路三八六號
發行所	三民書局股份有限公司 地址／臺北市復興北路三八六號 電話／二五〇〇六六〇〇 郵撥／〇〇〇九九九八——五號
印刷所	三民書局股份有限公司
門市部	復北店／臺北市復興北路三八六號 重南店／臺北市重慶南路一段六十一號
初　版	中華民國八十八年九月
編　號	S85481
定　價	新臺幣壹佰陸拾元整

行政院新聞局登記證局版臺業字第〇二〇〇號

有著作權‧不准侵害

ISBN　957–14–3013–7 (平裝)